INSIDE COLLEGE FOOTBALL

NOTRE DAME FIGHTING IRISH

BY WILLIAM MEIER

SportsZone

An Imprint of Abdo Publishing

abdobooks.com

abdobooks.com

Published by Abdo Publishing, a division of ABDO, PO Box 398166, Minneapolis, Minnesota 55439.

Printed in the United States of America, North Mankato, Minnesota
032020
092020

THIS BOOK CONTAINS RECYCLED MATERIALS

Cover Photo: AP Images
Interior Photos: Bettmann/Getty Images, 5; AP Images, 6, 8, 17, 19, 21, 27, 28, 43; Warner Bros./Hulton Archive/Archive Photos/Getty Images, 11; Frank Jansky/Icon Sportswire/Getty Images, 13; Harold Filan/AP Images, 22; Toby Massey/AP Images, 25; Tony Tomsic/AP Images, 31; Chuck Solomon/Sports Illustrated/Set Number: X32244 TK2 R3 F9/Getty Images, 32; John Swart/AP Images, 35; Dave Durohik/AP Images, 37; John Mersits/Cal Sport Media/AP Images, 39; John Bunch/Icon Sportswire/AP Images, 40

Editor: Patrick Donnelly
Series Designer: Nikki Nordby

Library of Congress Control Number: 2019954415

Publisher's Cataloging-in-Publication Data

Names: Meier, William, author.
Title: Notre Dame Fighting Irish / by William Meier
Description: Minneapolis, Minnesota : Abdo Publishing, 2021 | Series: Inside college football | Includes online resources and index.
Identifiers: ISBN 9781532192463 (lib. bdg.) | ISBN 9781644944684 (pbk.) | ISBN 9781098210366 (ebook)
Subjects: LCSH: Notre Dame Fighting Irish (Football team)--Juvenile literature. | Universities and colleges--Athletics--Juvenile literature. | American football--Juvenile literature. | College sports--United States--History--Juvenile literature.
Classification: DDC 796.33263--dc23

TABLE OF CONTENTS

CHAPTER 1

ROCKNE AND THE GIPPER

Knute Rockne eventually became one of the most influential people in college football history. But his arrival at the campus of the University of Notre Dame in South Bend, Indiana, in 1910 was much less heralded. Though he never finished high school, he had worked for several years to save money for college. As a 22-year-old freshman, Rockne stood just 5 feet 8 inches tall and weighed 160 pounds.

However, he became a valuable member of the Fighting Irish football team for four years. Rockne was the team captain in 1913. He was also an All-American that year. Notre Dame went 24–1–3 during his four seasons.

Rockne and quarterback Charles "Gus" Dorais dazzled opponents. Before they came along, few college teams used the

After serving as Notre Dame's captain, Knute Rockne became the team's legendary head coach.

Notre Dame coach Knute Rockne, *left*, instructs a player during practice in 1925. That team finished 7–2–1.

forward pass. It was starting to become a bigger weapon when they came along. Dorais and Rockne took it to another level.

Rockne was involved in a little bit of everything during his time as a student at Notre Dame. The Norway native wrote for the student yearbook and the newspaper. He was a part of the school orchestra, too, playing the flute. He played a major role in student plays. And he even got to the finals at a Notre Dame marbles tournament. Rockne was also an exceptional student who graduated with honors while studying chemistry.

It was coaching that gained Rockne his most fame, though. After graduating, he served as an assistant coach for four years under coach Jesse Harper. Then Rockne was named head coach in 1918. Rockne led the Fighting Irish for 13 years, from 1918 to 1930. He is still considered one of the best college football coaches of all time.

Rockne was a great motivator. He also designed some of the team's equipment. In addition, Rockne was the first coach to take his team around the country to play other teams. At the time most schools just played nearby opponents to save money. Notre Dame did play other Indiana teams. But the Fighting Irish also traveled from New York to Los Angeles to find quality opponents.

On the field, Rockne's teams were often among the country's best. He won 88 percent of his games. Through 2019, that was still the best winning percentage for any college or professional football coach. In all, Notre Dame won 105 games, lost 12, and tied five during Rockne's 13 years. In five of those seasons, Rockne led Notre Dame to an undefeated record. And the Irish were crowned national champions three times under Rockne—in 1924, 1929, and 1930.

HISTORY OF SUCCESS

Throughout college football history, few teams can match the success Notre Dame has had on the field. Through the 2019 season, just four schools had won more games than Notre Dame's 908. They were Michigan (962), Ohio State (924), Texas (916), and Alabama (916). The Irish had a winning percentage of .728. That was fourth all-time, trailing Ohio State (.730), Boise State (.729), and Michigan (.729). Notre Dame also had won 11 national titles.

Notre Dame's George Gipp was a top all-around football player. He rushed, passed, punted, and even played defensive back.

During his time at Notre Dame, Rockne coached some of the most famous players in college football history. Among them was George "The Gipper" Gipp. It is generally believed that

Rockne discovered Gipp while Rockne was still an assistant coach. Like Rockne, Gipp did not finish high school. He also arrived at Notre Dame as an older freshman in 1917. Gipp went to South Bend to play baseball. One day, Rockne saw Gipp drop-kicking a football for fun. Seeing the talent in the freshman, Rockne invited Gipp to try out for football.

Gipp was not the easiest player to manage. He liked the nightlife much more than he liked school. He often was late for practices—or he did not show up at all. But on the field, Gipp had few peers. By the time he was a senior in 1920, he was considered the best player in college football.

"I felt the thrill that comes to every coach when he knows it is his fate and his responsibility to handle unusual greatness . . . the perfect performer who comes rarely more than once in a generation," Rockne said of Gipp.

"He was a natural athlete. . . . And he possessed the three most important qualities needed to attain greatness: the qualities of body, mind, and spirit. He had what no coach or system can teach—football intuition."

Extremely athletic, Gipp could do it all. He led Notre Dame in rushing and passing during his final three seasons. He was a great punter. And he also was one of the best defensive backs the Irish have ever had. Even a century later, Gipp still holds a few Notre Dame records.

WIN ONE FOR THE GIPPER

Perhaps the most famous speech in sports history came from Knute Rockne. On November 10, 1928, Rockne's struggling Notre Dame team was preparing to face the favored Army team. George Gipp had died nearly eight years earlier. But according to Rockne, Gipp gave Rockne one final wish when he was dying.

To rally his team at halftime, Rockne delivered Gipp's words: "Some time, Rock, when the team is up against it, when things are wrong and the breaks are beating the boys—tell them to go in there with all they've got and win just one for the Gipper. I don't know where I'll be then, Rock. But I'll know about it. And I'll be happy."

The speech worked. Notre Dame came back at Yankee Stadium in New York that day and upset Army 12–6.

Rockne and Gipp both had a tremendous impact on Notre Dame football—and on college football, in general. Both of their lives ended in tragedy, too.

During Gipp's senior season, he became ill with strep throat that turned into pneumonia. He never recovered. On December 14, 1920—24 days after his last game—Gipp died. He was just 25 years old. Gipp's death was mourned around the country, and especially in South Bend and his hometown of Laurium, Michigan.

Nearly 11 years later, tragedy struck again. On March 31, 1931, Rockne boarded an airplane bound for Los Angeles. He was going there for a meeting about a football-themed movie. Shortly after takeoff, the plane flew into a storm. It crashed near Emporia, Kansas.

Future US President Ronald Reagan played George Gipp in the famous 1940 movie *Knute Rockne All-American*.

All eight people on the plane died. Rockne had turned 43 earlier that month.

Several legendary players and coaches have led the Irish to national championships in the decades that followed. Yet the legends of Rockne and Gipp are far from forgotten. Nearly a decade later, Ronald Reagan famously portrayed Gipp in a movie about Rockne's life, *Knute Rockne All-American*. They are still considered two of the greatest Notre Dame men ever.

CHAPTER 2

THE FOUR HORSEMEN

Michigan and Notre Dame are great rivals. They have played each other nearly every year since 1978. In fact, Notre Dame's first football game was against Michigan on November 23, 1887. However, the Wolverines came to South Bend to do more than just face off in a game against Notre Dame. They also made the trip to teach their competitors how to play football.

Michigan won that first game 8–0. Football in its early days hardly resembled the game played today. By most accounts, it was more similar to rugby than modern football. However, the game gradually evolved. And by 1924, Notre Dame was firmly established as one of the top college teams in the country.

The Irish finished with zero or one loss in 17 of 18 seasons between 1906 and 1923. Their worst record in those years was a 6–2 mark in 1914. The 1924 season, however, would go down as one of the greatest in school history. That year, the Irish won

The famous "Touchdown Jesus" mural is painted on Hesburgh Library near Notre Dame Stadium.

their first consensus national title. It came thanks in large part to a quartet of star players.

Jim Crowley, Elmer Layden, Don Miller, and Harry Stuhldreher were seniors on the 1924 team. They made up the Notre Dame backfield under coach Knute Rockne. Individually, each one of them was a great player.

Crowley was a fantastic runner and kicker. He led the Irish in scoring in 1924. Layden was faster than the other three. In addition to his running, Layden was the team's top kick returner. Stuhldreher was Notre Dame's quarterback, and he also returned punts. And in his career, Miller had more rushing yards than every player in Notre Dame history to that point except for one—the legendary George Gipp. Miller was the team's top runner and receiver in 1924.

Today each one of those four players is enshrined in the College Football Hall of Fame. Together, they will forever be known as "the Four Horsemen."

In 1924, the Four Horsemen led Notre Dame to a 10–0 record and the school's first national championship. The key win that season—and the key moment in the legend of the Four Horsemen—came on October 18, 1924, at the Polo Grounds in New York. That day, the Irish played the powerful Army team. Layden scored a touchdown in the first half. Crowley added another one in the second half. And Notre Dame went on to win 13–7. It was Army's only loss all season.

After the game, famous sportswriter Grantland Rice wrote about it for the *New York Herald-Tribune*. The lead of his story

BACK-TO-BACK CHAMPIONS

The 1924 season was the first national championship season for Notre Dame. The Irish would go on to win two more under coach Knute Rockne. In 1929 All-Americans Frank Carideo and Jack Cannon led the Irish to a 9–0 record. The next season, Carideo and Marchy Schwartz were two of the team's best players in a 10–0 season. The Irish were crowned national champions after both seasons.

During that 19-game stretch, Notre Dame outscored its opponents 410–112. Carideo, Cannon, and Schwartz have all been inducted into the College Football Hall of Fame. Three other Hall of Famers also were a part of at least one of those two championship teams: Frank Hoffmann, Bert Metzger, and Tommy Yarr.

is still considered one of the greatest pieces of work in sports journalism history:

"Outlined against a blue-gray October sky, the Four Horsemen rode again," he wrote. "In dramatic lore they are known as Famine, Pestilence, Destruction, and Death. These are only aliases. Their real names are Stuhldreher, Miller, Crowley, and Layden. They formed the crest of the South Bend cyclone before which another fighting Army football team was swept over the precipice at the Polo Grounds yesterday afternoon as 55,000 spectators peered down on the bewildering panorama spread on the green plain below."

Shortly after that famous game, Notre Dame student publicity aide George Strickler had an idea. He got the four players to pose while sitting atop horses. The photo is still one of the most famous in sports history.

Notre Dame was selected to play in the Rose Bowl after that season, on January 1, 1925. The Rose Bowl is the oldest bowl game, and it remains among the most important. In that 1925 game, the Irish defeated Stanford 27–10. That win clinched the national championship. However, it was the first—and only—bowl game in which the Irish played before 1969.

From 1922 through 1924, the Four Horsemen dominated Notre Dame opponents. But it was on that October day against Army that they became legendary.

None of the Four Horsemen was taller than 6 feet. None weighed more than 165 pounds, either. Yet, nearly a century later, they remain among the giants in college football history. Together they played 30 games, going 27–2–1. The only team to beat them was Nebraska, which did so twice.

Following their playing careers, the Four Horsemen all went into coaching. Layden coached the Irish to a 47–13–3 record from 1934

NOTRE DAME STADIUM

On October 4, 1930, the Irish opened Notre Dame Stadium. Marchy Schwartz scored the game-winning touchdown with four minutes to play in that inaugural game. The score lifted the Irish past Southern Methodist University (SMU) 20–14. In 1930, the stadium cost $750,000 to build. About $50 million was then spent in 1997 to expand the stadium, which now seats approximately 78,000 fans. Before 2019, every game since Thanksgiving Day in 1973 against Air Force had been a sellout. The streak ended on November 16, 2019, when fans failed to purchase every ticket for a game against Navy.

Notre Dame's Four Horsemen pose on horses in this famous photo following the 1924 game against Army.

to 1940. One of those wins came at Ohio State on November 2, 1935. Notre Dame scored with 32 seconds left to upset the Buckeyes 18–13. It was one of the most famous games of its time.

From its humble beginnings in 1887 through 1930, Notre Dame played some great football and had some great players. Nothing, however, could compare to the Four Horsemen and the 1924 national championship squad.

CHAPTER 3

SETTING A STANDARD

Notre Dame had the best team in college football in 1949. On the final day of the season, however, the Irish found themselves in a battle. Notre Dame had a 27–20 lead against the SMU Mustangs on December 3, 1949. Time was running out, but SMU quarterback Kyle Rote had his team in position for an upset.

Rote and the Mustangs had marched all the way down the field. Now they were just four yards from a touchdown. With time for one more play, Rote tried a jump pass into the end zone. But instead of reaching an SMU receiver, the ball landed in the hands of Irish linebacker Jerry Groom. That gave Notre Dame the win—and another national title. It also capped off one of the greatest decades in college football history.

Notre Dame was usually one of the country's best teams. But in the 1940s, under the direction of coach Frank Leahy, the Irish

Linebacker Jerry Groom intercepted a pass against SMU to seal Notre Dame's 1949 national championship.

were nearly unstoppable. Leahy had great success on the football field. That makes sense given the name of his hometown—Winner, South Dakota. Leahy played tackle at Notre Dame from 1928 to 1930. As a player, he won two national titles under coach Knute Rockne. And in 1941, Leahy became Notre Dame's head coach.

Leahy had instant success. He went 8–0–1 in his first season. Then he led the Irish to the 1943 national title with a 9–1–0 record. Leahy missed the next two seasons as he served in the US Navy during World War II (1939–1945). But he resumed his position as head coach in 1946. Starting that season, the Irish went four straight years without losing a game. From 1946 to 1949, they went 36–0–2 and won three national championships. The only blemishes were a scoreless tie with No. 1 Army in 1946 and a 14–14 tie at Southern California (USC) in 1948.

In 1947 quarterback John Lujack won the Heisman Trophy, which is rewarded to the nation's best college football best player. Lujack and All-America tackle George Connor led the Irish to the 1946 and 1947 national titles.

FIRST HEISMAN

In 1943 quarterback Angelo Bertelli helped Notre Dame win the national title and became the first Heisman Trophy winner in school history. He played in just six games but threw for more than 500 yards and 10 touchdowns. Then Bertelli left to serve in the Marines during World War II. Weeks later, he was going through boot camp in Parris Island, South Carolina, when he listened on the radio to Notre Dame's upset loss against Great Lakes. "I left the room crying and when I went outside, that's when I was handed the telegram that I had won the Heisman," he said.

Quarterbacks Angelo Bertelli, *left*, and John Lujack each won the Heisman Trophy while playing for Notre Dame.

The last of those titles was won in 1949 when Notre Dame beat SMU. The Irish finished the season 10–0. All-Americans Emil Sitko, Jim Martin, Bob Williams, and Leon Hart led the team. Hart won that year's Heisman Trophy.

"This is the greatest team I ever coached," Leahy said of the 1949 team. "Don't you think it must be the finest we have had at Notre Dame?"

Notre Dame's Heisman Trophy–winning quarterback Paul Hornung runs during a 1956 game against Southern California.

As great as the 1949 team was, Leahy knew many of his best players were graduating. Shortly after beating SMU, he said, "We will lose five games next year." He was almost right. The Irish went 4–4–1 in 1950.

The losing did not last long, though. Notre Dame was able to add more talented players over the next couple years. In 1953 Leahy and the Irish finished 9–0–1 and ranked second in the nation. That was his last season, however. And tough times were ahead.

From 1954 to 1963, three men took turns as Notre Dame's coach. The Irish went 51–48 during those 10 seasons. From 1889 to 1955, the Irish had only had one losing season. They then had three from 1956 to 1963. One of the most memorable games during those years came on November 16, 1957. That day, the Fighting Irish visited No. 1 Oklahoma. The Sooners had won 47 games in a row—a record that still stood more than 60 years later. On this day, however, Notre Dame came out on top to end Oklahoma's winning streak. Dick Lynch scored the only touchdown in a 7–0 victory.

GOLDEN BOY WINS HEISMAN

There was not much Paul Hornung could not do. Hornung, nicknamed "the Golden Boy," had his best season in 1956. That year, he led Notre Dame in rushing, passing, scoring, and return yards. In addition, he played defense and was the Irish place-kicker. As great as he was, though, the Irish won just two of their 10 games. Still, Hornung was recognized as the Heisman Trophy winner. Through 2019 he was still the only player from a losing team to win the award. After college, Hornung had a Hall of Fame career with the Green Bay Packers of the National Football League (NFL).

Eventually, the glory days would return to Notre Dame. But nothing could match the run of success that Leahy and his teams had in the 1940s.

CHAPTER 4

THE TRADITION GROWS

Notre Dame was in need of a change following a disappointing 2–7 season in 1963. The school hoped Ara Parseghian could restore the winning tradition. Parseghian, who took over in 1964, was different from all previous Notre Dame head coaches. He was the first who had not previously played for the Fighting Irish. He was also the first head coach to lead the Catholic institution who did not practice that religion. It didn't take long for Parseghian to show he was the right guy for the job, though.

In his first season, Parseghian led the Irish to a 9–1 record and a number three national ranking. By his third year, the Fighting Irish again were national champions.

Perhaps the biggest game in Parseghian's time in South Bend resulted not in a win, but a tie. On November 19, 1966, No. 1 Notre Dame visited No. 2 Michigan State. More than 80,000 fans

Notre Dame coach Ara Parseghian talks with quarterback Terry Hanratty on the sidelines during a 1967 game.

filled Spartan Stadium in East Lansing, Michigan. Another 33 million watched on television.

Michigan State jumped out to a 10–0 lead. But Notre Dame tied it early in the fourth quarter. And the game remained tied with 1:24 left to play. By then several of Notre Dame's best players had been injured. A tough wind whipped through the stadium, too. So Parseghian decided to run down the clock and settle for a 10–10 tie. Many people questioned his decision to not go for the win. However, the Irish came out the next week and crushed USC 51–0. That secured the Irish's first national championship in 17 years.

HUARTE'S HEISMAN

Of the Notre Dame players to win a Heisman Trophy, none were as surprising as John Huarte. He rarely played before his senior season in 1964. As a junior, he was the third-string quarterback. Ara Parseghian made Huarte the starter in Parseghian's first season. The California native shined. Huarte set 12 school records that season and led the Irish to a 9–1 record. Senior wide receiver Jack Snow finished fifth in Heisman balloting that year.

"That was one of the most beautiful football games that has ever been played," Parseghian said after the tie with Michigan State. "What the writers and the general public wanted was a winner out of this ballgame. The strategy that we employed is one that I have absolutely no regret about."

All-Americans Nick Eddy, Jim Lynch, Tom Regner, and Alan Page led that 1966 squad. Twelve Notre Dame players earned some sort of All-America recognition that year. That was more than in any

Notre Dame running back Bob Gladieux dives over Southern California defenders during a 1968 game.

other year in school history. It was one of the most dominating Notre Dame teams ever. That season, the Irish outscored their 10 opponents 362–38. Six teams failed to score a single point on the Irish defense.

The 1969 and 1970 squads did not win national titles. They did get to bowl games, though. Notre Dame's only bowl appearance to that point had been the Rose Bowl after the 1924 season. Led by star quarterback Joe Theismann, the Irish went to the Cotton Bowl after

Notre Dame quarterback Joe Theismann runs with the ball during a 1970 game against Purdue.

the 1969 and 1970 seasons. Notre Dame played Texas in both games. And Texas entered each game ranked number one in the nation.

The Longhorns won the first battle 21–17. In the second, Theismann led the Irish to a 24–11 upset win in his final college game. Theismann threw for 176 yards and a touchdown. He also ran for two touchdowns. Notre Dame finished 10–1 and was ranked number two in the country. Theismann went on to a stellar professional career.

The Irish had just two All-Americans in 1973. They were senior tight end Dave Casper and senior defensive back Mike Townsend. Yet behind Casper, Townsend, and junior quarterback Tom Clements, Notre Dame finished 11–0. The Irish secured the national championship with a 24–23 win over Alabama in the Sugar Bowl. That 1973 team had the fewest All-Americans of any of Notre Dame's 11 national championship teams.

Parseghian coached one more year in South Bend before retiring. He had an 11-year record of 95–17–4. His Irish teams won two national titles and finished ranked in the top 10 nine times. For that, he was inducted into the College Football Hall of Fame in 1980.

Notre Dame hired Dan Devine as Parseghian's replacement. Devine had previously coached at Arizona State and Missouri and for the Green Bay Packers of the NFL. His task was simple: just keep winning.

RUDY!

One of the most famous players in Notre Dame history hardly ever played for the Irish. Daniel "Rudy" Ruettiger came from a large family in Joliet, Illinois. He grew up watching Notre Dame football and dreamed of one day playing for the Irish. Ruettiger was a good player in high school. However, most college coaches considered him to be too small to play at that level. In addition, Ruettiger did not initially get into Notre Dame.

After two years of hard work at nearby Holy Cross College, Ruettiger got accepted by Notre Dame. He managed to make the football team as a practice player in 1974 and 1975. Finally, in the last home game of the 1975 season, Ruettiger was allowed to dress in uniform. In the last minute of a 24–3 win over Georgia Tech, he got to play for the first—and only—time. His story was told in a 1993 movie called *Rudy*.

CHAPTER 5

TOP OF THE CLASS

Notre Dame's prospects did not always look bright in 1977. The Irish lost their second game of the year to Mississippi 20–13. That dropped them to number 11 in the national rankings. But the Irish came back to win their last nine regular-season games. On January 2, 1978, the fifth-ranked Irish faced No. 1 Texas in the Cotton Bowl.

Texas was the only unbeaten team in major college football that season. Yet prior to the game, Notre Dame junior linebacker Bob Golic made a bold prediction. "I think we are going to beat them soundly," he said. "In my opinion, it won't be a squeaker."

Notre Dame's defense was spectacular in 1977. In addition to Golic, the Irish featured senior defensive end Ross Browner. Some consider Browner to be the best defensive player in Notre Dame history. But Texas's powerful running back Earl Campbell had won

Notre Dame quarterback Joe Montana led the Fighting Irish into contention for the 1977 national title.

Allen Pinkett (20) was a workhorse for the Irish in his four years at South Bend.

the Heisman Trophy that year. Behind Campbell, Texas had one of the top offenses in the country that season.

In the Cotton Bowl, Notre Dame's defense won the battle. Campbell had a good day. But the Irish forced six Texas turnovers.

Notre Dame's offense had some stars of its own. Junior quarterback Joe Montana would go on to a Hall of Fame career while leading the San Francisco 49ers to four Super Bowl titles. Senior tight end Ken MacAfee was an All-American. Irish running backs junior Jerome Heavens (101 yards) and sophomore Vagas Ferguson (100 yards) both ran well against Texas. Ferguson scored three touchdowns. Montana threw for 111 yards and a touchdown.

When it was over, Notre Dame had won 38–10. That gave the Irish their tenth national title. Golic was named the game's Most Valuable Player on defense. "I just had to remind coach," Golic said, "that I was right all along."

Montana did not have his best day in the national title game. And he never did earn All-America honors. Yet it was at Notre Dame that he first became a legend. Perhaps his greatest individual moment for the Irish came the next season in his last college game.

PINKETT RACKS UP YARDS

From 1982 to 1985, Allen Pinkett was a star running back for the Irish. He ended his college career as the school's all-time leader in rushing yards with 4,131. His 1,394 yards in 1983 has remained one of the best single-season totals in team history. He is also one of just two players in school history with three 1,000-yard seasons.

On January 1, 1979, Notre Dame was back in the Cotton Bowl against Houston. The weather was bitter cold. The day was miserable, and so was Montana's play. He was sick with the flu. Montana nearly missed the second half. But he drank some chicken soup and started feeling better, so he went back to the field late in the third quarter. The game came down to its final play. That is when Montana threw a touchdown pass to Kris Haines to give the Irish a 35–34 win.

Dan Devine resigned after the 1980 season to spend more time with his wife, who had become ill. In six years with Devine, the Irish went 53–16–1 and won a national title. The future looked bright for new coach Gerry Faust. However, over five seasons, things never quite clicked. His teams featured many star players, such as All-America linebacker Bob Crable, defensive back Dave Duerson, and running back Allen Pinkett. But the Irish never won more than seven games in a season under Faust. After the 1985 season, Lou Holtz was brought in to replace him.

By 1988 Holtz had built Notre Dame into a strong team. The Irish entered the season ranked among the top 15. Led by dual-threat junior quarterback Tony Rice, freshman wide receiver Raghib "The Rocket" Ismail, and a defense featuring four All-Americans, Notre Dame started piling up wins.

BROWN CAPTURES HEISMAN

In 1987 wide receiver Tim Brown became the seventh Notre Dame player to win the Heisman Trophy. A great receiver and kick returner, he actually had a better year statistically in 1986. But in 1987, he was sixth in the country with 167.9 all-purpose yards per game. He easily won the Heisman voting. Following college, Brown had a successful NFL career as a receiver and returner, playing mostly with the Los Angeles/Oakland Raiders. Brown was elected to the College Football Hall of Fame in 2009.

The Irish did have a couple close calls. They needed a late push to beat Michigan in the opener. Then in October, they faced a tough test against top-ranked Miami. Notre Dame jumped to a 21–7 lead. But Miami came back and scored a touchdown with 45 seconds left. That made it 31–30 in favor of Notre Dame. Miami decided to go for a two-point conversion after the touchdown. But the pass was incomplete and the Irish held on to win. Before long they had completed the regular season 11–0.

Behind quarterback Tony Rice, Notre Dame's 1988 team was known as one of the best Fighting Irish squads ever.

On January 2, 1989, Notre Dame beat third-ranked West Virginia 34–21 in the Fiesta Bowl. That gave the Irish their eleventh national championship. Little did fans know, that would be their last one for a long time.

CHAPTER 6

A NEW ERA

The Irish have had good teams since their 1988 national title. Notre Dame was ranked as high as third at some point in five of the next six seasons. The Irish have had good players, too. Quarterback Rick Mirer and running backs Reggie Brooks and Jerome Bettis led a powerful Irish offense in the early 1990s. They just couldn't quite lead Notre Dame to another championship.

The Irish came agonizingly close twice. In 1989 they were undefeated going into the final regular-season game only to be upset by Miami. It was the same situation in 1993 when Boston College pulled off the upset. The Irish finished second both years.

Lou Holtz left Notre Dame after the 1996 season with a record of 100–30–2. Only Knute Rockne, with 105 victories, won more games as Notre Dame's coach. However, inconsistency awaited.

New coach Bob Davie lasted just five years. The team had losing records in two of them. In 2002 Tyrone Willingham became

Notre Dame running back Jerome Bettis runs into the end zone during a 1992 game against Penn State.

the first black head coach in Notre Dame history. The Irish went 10–3 in his first season, but just 11–12 in his last two. He was fired before the final game in 2004. Charlie Weis then took over from there.

The Irish had some success under Weis. Behind record-setting senior quarterback Brady Quinn, they won 10 games in 2006. At one point they were ranked as high as second in the nation. But they ended the year ranked No. 17. The Irish fell to 3–9 the next year. Two years after that, Weis was fired.

Notre Dame needed somebody to restore the tradition. The school turned to Brian Kelly, who had just led Cincinnati to an undefeated regular season.

"You do not come to the University of Notre Dame because you want to be average," Kelly said at his introductory news conference. "You want to be the best of the best. That's why I'm here."

The Irish set about getting there. And after 8–5 seasons in 2010 and 2011, they were ready to take the leap. Despite starting the season unranked, Notre Dame rode a dominant defense to win after win. Some games were really tight. Five times the Irish won by

FLOYD SETS RECORDS

Notre Dame has a history filled with great receivers. But Michael Floyd might be the best the Irish have ever had. He was a four-year starter from 2008 to 2011. Floyd set nearly every receiving record at Notre Dame. He finished with school records for career receptions (271), receiving yards (3,686), and touchdown catches (37). In 2011, Floyd had 1,147 yards on 100 catches, a school record for a single season.

All-America linebacker Manti Te'o led Notre Dame to the national title game after the 2012 season.

seven points or fewer. They needed overtime to beat Stanford and three overtimes to beat Pitt. But with linebacker Manti Te'o leading the way, the Irish finished the regular season 12–0.

That was enough to get Notre Dame into the National Championship Game. That game didn't even exist in 1988, when

Notre Dame players take the field for their Cotton Bowl game against Clemson in 2018.

champions were determined solely by polls of the media and coaches. Unfortunately for the Irish, that game was not close. On January 7, 2013, Alabama steamrolled Notre Dame 42–14.

Despite the sour ending, Notre Dame finished the season with its highest ranking in nearly two decades. And Notre Dame remained competitive in the coming years under Kelly. However, the Irish later had to forfeit their wins from 2012 and 2013 after breaking academics rules.

Meanwhile, Notre Dame in 2014 began a relationship with the Atlantic Coast Conference (ACC). While the Fighting Irish are full members in other sports, the football team plays some ACC teams each year while remaining an independent. That's allowed the team to continue its traditional rivalries with schools such as Michigan and USC that play in other conferences.

Besides a surprising 4–8 season in 2016, the Irish remained competitive. They went 10–3 in both 2015 and 2017. One year later, they were even better. Beating four ranked opponents, Notre Dame went 12–0 in the regular season. That earned the team its first berth into the four-team College Football Playoff, which had begun in the 2014 season. However, eventual national champion Clemson overpowered the Irish 30–3 in the Cotton Bowl semifinal.

They followed that season by going 11–2 and finishing with the No. 12 ranking in 2019. It wasn't a national title, but for Irish fans there was reason to be excited. After all of the turmoil of the late 1990s and early 2000s, Notre Dame was once again among the best teams in the nation.

MANTI TE'O

Senior linebacker Manti Te'o was Notre Dame's emotional leader in 2012. Te'o had grown up in Hawaii. He developed into an All-American in South Bend. He also finished second in voting for the Heisman Trophy. The 1,706 points Te'o got in the Heisman voting were the most points ever for a defense-only player.

Te'o also attracted some unwanted attention that season. A woman he believed he was in a long-distance relationship with supposedly died. Many media outlets covered the story. However, later it was revealed that his girlfriend wasn't real. Somebody had tricked Te'o in an elaborate hoax.

TIMELINE

1887
On November 23, Notre Dame plays its first football game, losing to Michigan 8–0.

1920
Coach Knute Rockne and star player George Gipp lead the Irish to a second straight 9–0 season. Shortly after the season, Gipp dies after complications from strep throat.

1924
Led by the famed Four Horsemen backfield, the Irish win their first national title.

1929
Rockne and quarterback Frank Carideo guide the Irish to a second national title.

1930
Notre Dame Stadium is dedicated, and the Irish celebrate their new home in style. They finish 10–0 and win a second straight national title.

1931
On March 31, Rockne is killed in a plane crash in Kansas. During his 13-year tenure as coach, the Irish went 105–12–5.

1943
Notre Dame wins its first national title with coach Frank Leahy, while quarterback Angelo Bertelli becomes the first Notre Dame player to win the Heisman Trophy.

1946
After missing the previous two seasons because of military service, Leahy returns to the team. He leads the Irish to their fifth national title.

1947
John Lujack wins Notre Dame's second Heisman Trophy. He also leads the Irish to their second straight national title.

1949
Leahy and the Irish win their third title in four years. Heisman Trophy winner Leon Hart leads the way.

1953
John Lattner, who does a little of everything on the field for Notre Dame, becomes the school's fourth Heisman Trophy winner.

1956
Notre Dame struggles to a 2–8 season, but Paul Hornung is a star. Hornung wins the Heisman Trophy to become the first player from a losing team to win the award.

1964
Quarterback John Huarte wins the Heisman Trophy, but a 20–17 loss at USC prevents the Irish from winning the national title.

1966
A famous tie with Michigan State helps Notre Dame stay at number one and win its eighth national title.

1973
With a one-point win over Alabama in the Sugar Bowl on December 31, the Irish win their ninth national title.

1977
Future Pro Football Hall of Fame quarterback Joe Montana guides the Irish to their tenth national title.

1987
Receiver/kick returner Tim Brown becomes the seventh Heisman Trophy winner in Notre Dame history.

1988
Coach Lou Holtz and quarterback Tony Rice steer Notre Dame to a 12–0 record and the eleventh national championship in school history.

2013
Notre Dame loses to Alabama in the national championship game on January 7.

2018
The Irish go undefeated in the regular season to qualify for the College Football Playoff. However, Clemson beats them 30–3 in a semifinal at the Cotton Bowl.

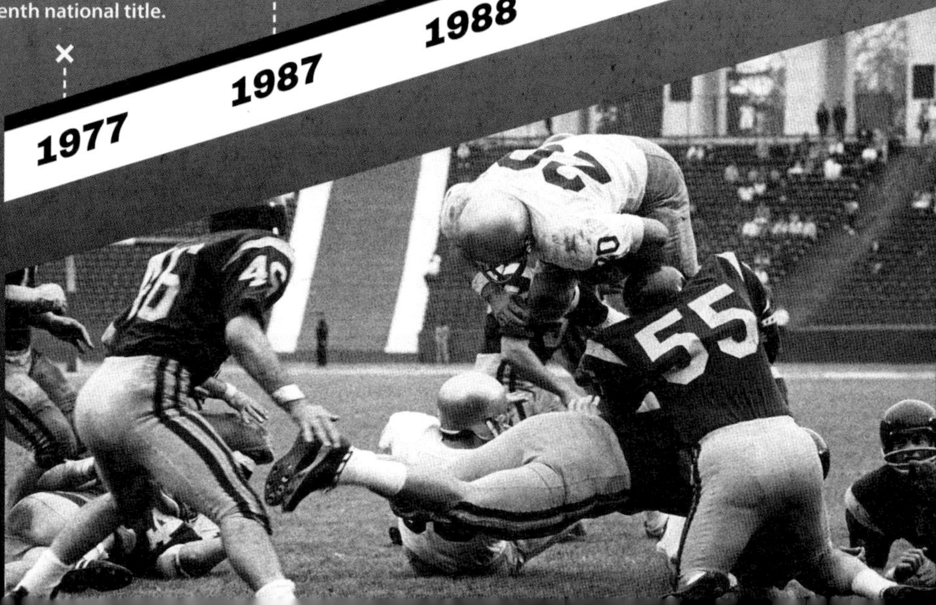

QUICK STATS

PROGRAM INFO

University of Notre Dame
Catholics, Hoosiers, Ramblers, Rockmen, Westerners (1887–1926)
University of Notre Dame
Fighting Irish (1927–)

NATIONAL CHAMPIONSHIPS

1924, 1929, 1930, 1943, 1946, 1947, 1949, 1966, 1973*, 1977, 1988

OTHER ACHIEVEMENTS

College Football Playoffs berths (2014–): 1
Bowl record: 19–19

KEY COACHES

Lou Holtz (1986–96)
100–30–2, 5–4 (bowl games)
Frank Leahy (1941–43, 1946–53)
87–11–9
Ara Parseghian (1964–74)
95–17–4, 3–2 (bowl games)
Knute Rockne (1918–30)
105–12–5, 1–0 (bowl games)

KEY PLAYERS

Angelo Bertelli (QB, 1941–43)**
Tim Brown (WR, 1984–87)**
Ross Browner (DE, 1973, 1975–77)
George Connor (T, 1946–47)
Bob Crable (LB, 1978–81)
Michael Floyd (WR, 2008–11)
George Gipp (HB, 1917–20)
Leon Hart (E/DE, 1946–49)**
Paul Hornung (QB/S, 1954–56)**
John Huarte (QB, 1962–64)**
Raghib Ismail (WR, 1988–90)
John Lattner (HB, 1951–53)**
John Lujack (QB, 1943, 1946–47)**
Joe Montana (QB, 1975, 77–78)
Alan Page (DE, 1964–66)
Tony Rice (QB, 1987–89)
Manti Te'o (LB, 2009–12)

HOME STADIUM

Notre Dame Stadium (1930–)

*Denotes shared title
**Heisman Trophy winner
All statistics through 2019 season

QUOTES AND ANECDOTES

Hesburgh Library sits just outside of Notre Dame Stadium. On the wall facing the stadium is a large mural of Jesus, surrounded by his followers. In the picture, Jesus is raising his arms—similar to how a referee would signal a touchdown. Although stadium expansion has largely blocked the view of the mural from inside, the mural will forever be known as "Touchdown Jesus."

Golics, Notre Dame, and broadcasting just seem to go together. Linebacker Bob Golic was a two-time All-American and starred on Notre Dame's 1977 national championship team. After he left, younger brother Greg Golic joined the team as an offensive lineman. He was soon joined by youngest brother Mike, a defensive end. Bob and Mike went on to play in the NFL and later became broadcasters. Meanwhile, Mike's son, Mike Golic Jr., played for the Irish in 2011. Mike Jr. later joined his dad at ESPN.

"I've been in a Super Bowl and I've played in front of a hundred thousand fans, but nothing in my 12-year NFL career ever compared to running out on the field at Notre Dame Stadium. It felt like my feet never touched the ground. To this day, I still get goosebumps just talking about it."

—Joe Theismann, Notre Dame quarterback, 1968 to 1970

Many Irish fans believed Raghib "The Rocket" Ismail should have won the Heisman Trophy in 1990. Ismail was a great receiver who also electrified the crowd with his punt and kick returns. He is the only player in college football history through 2019 to score touchdowns on two kickoff returns in two separate games. He finished as runner-up in the 1990 Heisman Trophy

GLOSSARY

All-American
Designation for athletes chosen as the best college players in the country in a particular sport.

consensus
Unanimous agreement.

forfeit
Forced to give up, often due to breaking a rule.

inducted
To be ceremoniously admitted to a position or place, such as the Hall of Fame.

legend
An extremely famous person, especially in a particular field.

ranking
A national position as determined by voters.

rival
An opponent with whom a player or team has a fierce and ongoing competition.

two-point conversion
An option for teams that have scored a touchdown to try a running or passing play from the 2-yard line for two points, instead of kicking for one point.

upset
An unexpected victory by a supposedly weaker team or player.

MORE INFORMATION

BOOKS

Temple, Ramey. *Notre Dame Fighting Irish*. New York: AV2 by Weigl, 2020.

Wilner, Barry. *The Story of the College Football National Championship Game*. Minneapolis, MN: Abdo Publishing, 2016.

York, Andy. *Ultimate College Football Road Trip*. Minneapolis, MN: Abdo Publishing, 2019.

ONLINE RESOURCES

Booklinks NONFICTION NETWORK FREE! ONLINE NONFICTION RESOURCES

To learn more about the Notre Dame Fighting Irish, please visit **abdobooklinks.com** or scan this QR code. These links are routinely monitored and updated to provide the most current information available.

PLACES TO VISIT

College Football Hall of Fame
cfbhall.com

This hall of fame and museum in Atlanta, Georgia, highlights the greatest players and moments in the history of college football. Among the former Fighting Irish enshrined here are Knute Rockne, George Gipp, Paul Hornung, Alan Page, and Tim Brown.

Notre Dame Stadium
und.com/facilities-notre-dame-stadium

This has been Notre Dame's home field since 1930

INDEX

ABOUT THE AUTHOR

William Meier has worked as an author and editor in the publishing industry for more than 25 years. He resides in St. Louis, Missouri, with his wife and their poodle, Macy.